W9-ATM-354

Dear Parent:
Your child's love of reading starts here!

Every child learns to read in a different way and at his or her own speed. Some go back and forth between reading levels and read favorite books again and again. Others read through each level in order. You can help your young reader improve and become more confident by encouraging his or her own interests and abilities. From books your child reads with you to the first books he or she reads alone, there are I Can Read Books for every stage of reading:

SHARED READING
Basic language, word repetition, and whimsical illustrations, ideal for sharing with your emergent reader

BEGINNING READING
Short sentences, familiar words, and simple concepts for children eager to read on their own

READING WITH HELP
Engaging stories, longer sentences, and language play for developing readers

READING ALONE
Complex plots, challenging vocabulary, and high-interest topics for the independent reader

ADVANCED READING
Short paragraphs, chapters, and exciting themes for the perfect bridge to chapter books

I Can Read Books have introduced children to the joy of reading since 1957. Featuring award-winning authors and illustrators and a fabulous cast of beloved characters, I Can Read Books set the standard for beginning readers.

A lifetime of discovery begins with the magical words "I Can Read!"

*Visit www.icanread.com for information
on enriching your child's reading experience.*

WALT DISNEY PICTURES AND WALDEN MEDIA PRESENT "THE CHRONICLES OF NARNIA: THE LION, THE WITCH AND THE WARDROBE" BASED ON THE BOOK BY C.S. LEWIS
A MARK JOHNSON PRODUCTION AN ANDREW ADAMSON FILM MUSIC COMPOSED BY HARRY GREGSON-WILLIAMS COSTUME DESIGNER ISIS MUSSENDEN EDITED BY SIM EVAN-JONES PRODUCTION DESIGNER ROGER FORD
DIRECTOR OF PHOTOGRAPHY DONALD M. McALPINE, ASC, ACS CO-PRODUCER DOUGLAS GRESHAM EXECUTIVE PRODUCERS ANDREW ADAMSON PERRY MOORE
WALDEN MEDIA SCREENPLAY BY ANN PEACOCK AND ANDREW ADAMSON AND CHRISTOPHER MARKUS & STEPHEN McFEELY PRODUCED BY MARK JOHNSON PHILIP STEUER DIRECTED BY ANDREW ADAMSON Walt Disney Pictures
Distributed by BUENA VISTA PICTURES DISTRIBUTION THE CHRONICLES OF NARNIA, NARNIA, and all book titles, characters and locales original to The Chronicles of C.S. Lewis Pte Ltd. and are used with permission. ©Disney Enterprises, Inc. and Walden Media, LLC. All rights reserved.

Narnia.com

The Lion, the Witch and the Wardrobe: Welcome to Narnia

Copyright © 2005 by C.S. Lewis Pte. Ltd.

The Chronicles of Narnia®, Narnia® and all book titles, characters
and locales original to The Chronicles of Narnia are trademarks of C.S. Lewis Pte. Ltd.
Use without permission is strictly prohibited.

Photographs © 2005 Disney Enterprises, Inc. and Walden Media, LLC.

Photographs by Phil Bray, Richard Corman and Donald M. McAlpine

HarperCollins®, ®, and I Can Read Book® are trademarks of HarperCollins Publishers.

Library of Congress catalog card number: 2004117933.

Printed in the United States of America.

For information address HarperCollins Children's Books, a division of HarperCollins Publishers,
1350 Avenue of the Americas, New York, NY 10019.

Book design by Rick Farley

❖

WELCOME TO NARNIA

Adapted by Jennifer Frantz

Based on the screenplay by
Ann Peacock and Andrew Adamson and
Christopher Markus & Stephen McFeely

Based on the book by C. S. Lewis

Directed by Andrew Adamson

HarperCollins*Publishers*

The Pevensie family never dreamed that a magic wardrobe would change their lives!

Lucy was the first Pevensie to find
out the secret inside the wardrobe.

She and her brothers and sister were playing hide-and-seek.
Lucy needed a place to hide!
She dashed inside a wardrobe in an otherwise empty room.

As Lucy moved toward the back of the wardrobe, she felt a cold wind. What was going on?

That was when Lucy discovered Narnia—a magical land full of snow and different, wonderful creatures!

Later, Lucy shared her discovery.
At first no one believed Lucy's story
about Narnia.

Peter, Susan and Edmund thought she
was just playing a game.
How could there be another whole world
in the back of a wardrobe?
But soon the other Pevensie children would
visit Narnia, too.

Lucy was the youngest in the family.
She loved to read and have adventures.
Lucy also liked to make new friends . . .

. . . like Mr. Tumnus, the Faun.
She met him on her first trip to Narnia.

Edmund was the second of the Pevensie
children to visit Narnia.
At first he teased his sister Lucy.
Then he found out her story was true.
But while Lucy made nice friends
when she went to Narnia,
Edmund did not.

You see, Edmund had a way of finding trouble wherever he went.

And that was what he found in Narnia! Just after entering the land beyond the wardrobe, Edmund met the White Witch. She was the evil Queen of Narnia.

The White Witch gave Edmund
some enchanted candy called Turkish Delight.
He quickly fell under her spell.

Peter and Susan, the oldest children, were the last to visit Narnia.

They could not believe their eyes!

At first Susan was worried that her family might be in danger in Narnia. She thought it would be safer to go home.

But as time went by,
Susan grew to love Narnia.
She was a fierce protector of Narnia
and its creatures.

Peter, the oldest, always tried to protect his family and keep them together.

Peter tried to protect his family
in Narnia, too.
It was a lot of responsibility,
but as the oldest,
Peter knew it was his job.

The great Aslan saw how Peter took care
of his brother and sisters.
Aslan saw the bravery inside Peter.

He asked Peter to help him lead the creatures
of Narnia against the White Witch.
They worked together and freed Narnia.

The Pevensie family never dreamed
of the adventures they would have . . .

. . and the many creatures they would meet.

Or that they would later become
Kings and Queens of the magical place
called Narnia!

Peter the Magnificent
Susan the Gentle
Edmund the Just
Lucy the Valiant

Though they returned to their home eventually, Peter, Edmund, Susan and Lucy always kept Narnia in their hearts!